Barbie™ GIRLS CLUB

LET'S BE FRIENDS

BY SARAH JANE BRIAN

PHOTOGRAPHY: WILLY LEW, LYN CARLSON, GREG ROCCIA, JEREMY LLOYD, LISA COLLINS, AND JUDY TSUNO

A GOLDEN BOOK • NEW YORK

Golden Books Publishing Company, Inc.,
New York, New York 10106

WHAT'S INSIDE?

Catie

Best
Friends
Club

Use this as your guide!

BEST FRIENDS

It was school vacation time! Stacie had been looking forward to it for weeks.

"Good morning, Stacie!" said Barbie cheerfully. "How are you enjoying your first day of vacation?"

"I'm rearranging my room," Stacie said. "Doesn't it look terrific so far? I'm reading a great book, too. But most of my friends are away. I miss them already, especially Janet. She went to the seashore."

"I have an idea," said Barbie. "A new family moved into a house on Elm Street last week. One of the sisters, Amanda, is your age. Would you like to meet her?"

Stacie's face brightened. "Sure!" she said, jumping up.

MOST OF MY FRIENDS ARE AWAY. I MISS THEM ALREADY.

When Stacie and Barbie arrived, Amanda was in the backyard cleaning out a shed.

"My parents said I could decorate this shed and make it a clubhouse," Amanda explained after Barbie introduced the girls.

"I love decorating," said Stacie. "Do you need any help?"

"That would be great!" Amanda replied eagerly. "You can be the club's first member!"

"YOU CAN BE THE CLUB'S FIRST MEMBER!"

BEST FRIENDS CLUB

For the next two weeks, Amanda and Stacie met at the clubhouse every day. They put a sign over the door and hung curtains. Barbie even gave them some old chairs and a table.

Before long, the clubhouse looked perfect. Amanda gazed around the room, admiring their work. She turned to Stacie and smiled. "I'm glad I moved to this town," she said.

7

The next day, the girls were making club membership cards at Stacie's house when the phone rang. It was Janet!

"How was your trip? I'm so happy you're home!" cried Stacie into the phone. "You have got to come see my neighbor's clubhouse!"

But after Stacie hung up, she saw that Amanda was upset.

"How could you invite her to the clubhouse?" Amanda asked angrily. "I thought the Best Friends Club was for you and me. But I guess you don't want to be my friend now that Janet is back."

"That's ridiculous!" said Stacie. "Amanda . . ."

But Amanda was already running home.

9

Stacie and Barbie went to the park the next day.
"Isn't that Amanda by the swings?" asked Barbie.
"It sure is," said Stacie sadly.
"Why don't we go say hello?" suggested
Barbie. "I have a feeling you're
both ready to make up."
"I guess I am ready,"
Stacie said, starting off
across the playground.

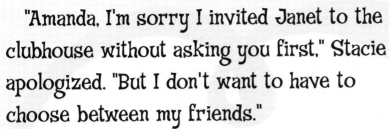

"Amanda, I'm sorry I invited Janet to the clubhouse without asking you first," Stacie apologized. "But I don't want to have to choose between my friends."

Amanda was still unhappy. "I know you feel hurt," Barbie told her. "But I think you should give Janet a chance. Who knows? She could become a great new friend to you, just like Stacie."

" SHE COULD BECOME A GREAT NEW FRIEND. "

That afternoon, Stacie and Janet went over to Amanda's house.

"I have something for you," Janet told Amanda, reaching into a bag she was carrying. "It's from my trip. I hope you like saltwater taffy!"

The girls picked their favorite flavors. Then they made lemonade and brought it out to the clubhouse.

"Wow! This clubhouse is so pretty!" said Janet. "You two did a great job."

"Thanks!" said Amanda and Stacie together.

"Now I have a surprise," Amanda said, handing Janet her very own club membership card. Janet's name sparkled in purple glitter.

"THIS CLUBHOUSE IS SO PRETTY!"

BEST FRIENDS CLUB

"Cool!" exclaimed Janet. "I'd love to be in your club."

Amanda grinned. "Barbie was right," she admitted shyly. "I think I almost missed out on a new friend."

CLUB CARDS

Make membership cards, just like the girls in the Best Friends Club!

You need:

- Colorful index cards
- Small stickers
- Glitter glue pens
- Small photo of yourself
- Glue
- Feathers, buttons, lace

What to do:

1. Make a border around the edges of your card with small heart or star stickers.

2. Glue a small photo of yourself to the card.

3. Use a glitter pen to write your name and your club name on the card.

4. If you like, glue on colored feathers, old buttons, pieces of lace, or whatever you can think of!

PRETTY PALS

Stacie and her friends love trying new hairstyles. Here's how they turn it into a game!

1. Each friend brings her own comb, brush, clips, and scrunchies.

2. Everyone sits in a circle and turns left.

3. Each girl creates a cool new do for the girl in front of her!

Barbie always has great styling ideas. Check out the pictures on this page! And remember, never share brushes or other hair stuff.

Make mini-ponies out of small sections of hair.

Twist two ponytails and secure with colorful clips.

Part your friend's hair and clip it back with a barrette or two!

DEAR BARBIE

Dear Barbie,

Last Saturday I asked my friend to go swimming, but she said she had to go to her grandma's house. I went to the mall with my mom instead. Guess who I saw? My friend with another girl!

I'm so mad, I don't know if I can ever forgive her. What should I do?

—Seeing Red

Dear Seeing Red,

It's awful to feel betrayed by a friend. But don't jump to conclusions before you know the whole story. Maybe there is an explanation for what you saw! For instance, your friend's grandmother could have come down with the flu. Or maybe your friend doesn't know how to swim and was embarrassed to tell you. Talk to your friend and listen to what she has to say. It could save your friendship!

Your friend,

Barbie

FASHION FUN PARTY

To celebrate their new Best Friends Club, Amanda had a glamorous dress-up party for her friends. You can have one, too!

Ask each guest to bring 3 or 4 skirts, shirts, dresses, or other pieces of clothing. Take turns putting together a cool outfit by mixing and matching your friends' clothes with yours. Then put on music and hold a fashion show!

18

FRIENDSHIP TEES

 Barbie had another great fashion idea. Try this craft with your friends!

You need:

- One plain white T-shirt for each girl (Get permission first!)
- Colored fabric paint (available at craft stores)
- White tissue paper
- Large grocery or garbage bags

What to do:

1. Cover the work area with a clean, unfolded bag or large piece of plastic.

2. Put tissue paper inside each shirt to keep the paint from soaking through.

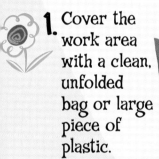

3. Use paint to sign your name on all of the shirts, and ask your friends to do the same. You can draw pictures, too!

4. Let dry for 24 hours. Then try on the shirts to see how they look!

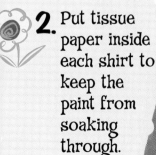

HOW WELL DO YOU KNOW

Write your answers on a separate sheet of paper. Check with your friend to see how many you got right. Then it's her turn!

Do you know...

1. your friend's favorite color?

2. her birthday?

3. her best school subject?

4. the last movie she saw?

5. her favorite song?

"THE MOST FUN I HAD WITH MY BEST FRIEND WAS WHEN WE WERE RIDING PONIES TOGETHER."
—DESARIAH, AGE 5

YOUR BEST FRIEND?

6. which stuffed animal she loves most?

7. if she prefers vanilla or chocolate?

8. what she wants to be when she grows up?

9. her favorite thing to do on vacation?

10. where her dream birthday party would be?

If you answered:

8 to 10 right: Wow! Are you sure you're not twins?

4 to 7 right: You know your friend pretty well, but she still surprises you once in a while.

0 to 3 right: You have a few things to learn about your friend, but that's okay! It's a good excuse to spend lots of time together.

MAKE AN ICE-CREAM

Try this recipe with a
pal or with a bunch
of buddies.

You need:

A few flavors of ice cream or frozen yogurt
Toppings, such as fresh or frozen berries, raisins,
chocolate syrup, whipped cream, chocolate candies,
and sprinkles.

What to do:

Make a sundae for a friend! Pick the ice cream
and toppings you think your friend would like
best. Barbie's favorite flavor is strawberry!
Be artistic. Use the toppings to make designs or
even a face on top of the sundae.

Tip:

Is your friend a picky eater? Before you start,
ask what flavors and toppings she *doesn't* like.

FRIEND-AE!

"I LIKE TO PLAY SCIENTIST AND INVENT THINGS WITH MY FRIENDS."
—CATIE, AGE 9

23

BARBIE'S TOP 5

Check out Barbie's five favorite things to do with her friends!

 1. Giggling on the phone on a rainy day.

 2. Walking our dogs together in the park.

 3. Offering a shoulder to lean on when times are tough.

4. Trying on each other's clothes.

 **"WE LIKE TO DRESS UP AND DANCE TO MUSIC."** —BIANCA, AGE 8

 5. Cheering each other on!

What are your favorite things to do with your friends?